Meet the Wolfy Kids!

Based on the episode "The Wolfy Kids"

SIMON SPOTLIGHT
An imprint of Simon & Schuster Children's Publishing Division
New York   London   Toronto   Sydney   New Delhi
1230 Avenue of the Americas, New York, New York 10020
This Simon Spotlight paperback edition August 2019

For information about special discounts for bulk purchases, please contact
Simon & Schuster Special Sales at 1-866-506-1949 or business@simonandschuster.com.
Manufactured in the United States of America 0919 LAK
4 6 8 10 9 7 5 3
ISBN 978-1-5344-5086-8 (pbk) • ISBN 978-1-5344-5087-5 (eBook)

Connor, Greg, and Amaya are walking outside to paint a wall in their schoolyard.

Connor is excited. "It'll be the best painting ever!" he says.

"We're painting a whole wall?" Greg asks, carrying two full cans of paint.

"With Connor's design," Amaya points out. "He won the competition!"

"I call it . . . Wallcat," Connor says proudly. He shows Amaya and Greg his winning design.

Suddenly Connor notices something on the wall that he was going to paint!

"Nooo!" Connor cries.

"Look—paw prints. Who did this?" Amaya asks.

"Sorry, kids. We can't paint today. Someone has messed up the wall," their teacher announces.

Connor is upset he won't get to paint his design on the wall.

"How about we do something else to make up for it?" Greg asks, trying to cheer up his friend.

They agree to check out the new comic books at the library!

A few minutes later Connor, Greg, and Amaya discover more paw prints at the library!

"Someone's ruining everyone's fun," Gekko says.

"This ends now!" Connor exclaims.

"PJ Masks, we're on our way! Into the night to save the day!" they all say together.

The PJ Masks head to the playground.

"Look—more paw prints. Looks like they belong to some kind of dogs . . . ," Owlette says.

"Who's doing this?" Catboy asks.

Suddenly the PJ Masks see glowing eyes from a dug-up hole in the playground.

"Maybe Romeo's made a furry dog robot?" Gekko wonders.

Just then some kids jump out of the hole.

"Yip-Yip-Yarooo!" they howl.

"Who are you?" Catboy asks.

"Me? I'm Howler," one of the kids replies.

"We're the Wolfy Kids, dude," another kid adds. "I'm Rip. And don't you forget it!"

"And you're . . . wolves?" Gekko asks nervously.

"We're *were-wolves*!" a third werewolf named Kevin roars.
"When the moon's out, we grow *fur*!" Rip says.
"When the moon's out, we grow *fangs*!" Howler adds.
"When the moon's out, we do *bad stuff*!" Rip finishes.

"You wrecked my art project, tore up the comics, and ruined the playground!" Catboy says.

"Every kid in the city is upset," Owlette adds. "Why did you do this?"

"We do what we want! We take what we want! This playground is ours! This whole town is ours!" Rip says.

"That's it!" yells Catboy.

Catboy uses his Super Cat Speed to charge around the Wolfy Kids.

"Ooh, speedy kitty-cat," Howler comments. "All set, Wolfy Kids?"

"*Yip-Yip-Yarooo!*" the Wolfy Kids howl together.

Their howl creates a giant sonic boom that sends the PJ Masks flying through the air! They land on the ground with a loud thump.

"The playground is ours, the town is ours, and now . . . the kitty-cat car is ours!" Howler declares, pointing at Catboy's Cat Car.

"But . . . it's mine!" Catboy yells.

"Not if you're not in our wolf pack," Rip tells him. "Come on, Howler. Let's wolf it up!"

The Wolfy Kids speed away in the Cat Car.

Catboy takes command, even though Gekko and Owlette want to make a plan first.

"PJ Robot! Activate the remote control on the Cat Car!" Catboy says.

PJ Robot starts to steer the Cat Car. Howler loses control!

"Oh no you don't, Mr. Wheely!" Howler roars. "With a huff and a puff—"

Clang!

The Cat Car swerves into a light post!

Back at HQ the remote control goes haywire, making the Cat Car bounce up and down. PJ Robot cannot fix it.

"We're jumping, guys!" Kevin cheers. "Jumping to . . . the *moon!*"

As the Cat Car approaches the moon with each bounce, the Wolfy Kids look up and start howling, as if in a trance.

"*Yarooo!*" they howl together.

"They said the moon changes them," Owlette says. "Maybe they think if they get closer to it—"

"More powers! More fur!" Kevin interrupts.

"My fangs will get bigger! My tail will get longer!" Howler adds.

"We've got to stop them now!" Catboy says.

The PJ Masks head to HQ. Catboy has a plan!

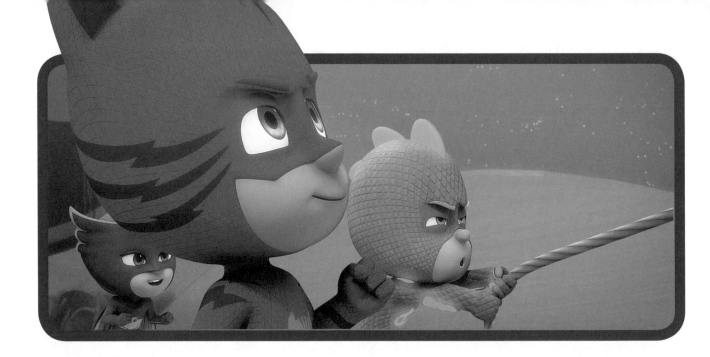

"Gekko, I need you to throw this at the Cat Car," Catboy says, handing him a rope.

Gekko uses his Super Gekko Muscles to throw the rope. It attaches to the Cat Car! PJ Robot spins HQ, pulling the Cat Car back inside.

"Fluttering feathers, I guess that did work!" Owlette says.

"Hey! You took our car!" Howler says to the PJ Masks.
"It's my car!" Catboy argues.
"Oh, yeah?" Rip says. "Why were we jumping to the moon in it then?"
"Scram out of our HQ!" Catboy tells them.

"Don't you get it?" Rip says. "Wherever we go and whatever we see is *ours!*"

"*Yip-Yip-Yarooo!*" The Wolfy Kids send a sonic howl at the PJ Masks.

The PJ Masks fly into the Picture Player as the Wolfy Kids race around HQ. The Wolfy Kids take the Owl Glider and the Gekko-Mobile. They want to go to the moon!

"This is fur-tastic!" Howler shouts.

"*Yarooo!*" the Wolfy Kids howl excitedly.

The PJ Masks jump into action.
"I guess we got your Cat Car back," Gekko says.
"But what about the Gekko-Mobile and the Owl Glider?"
Catboy asks.
"What about the *whole city*?" Owlette points out.
"You're right," Catboy admits. "I was just thinking of myself."

"Time to be a hero!" Catboy declares.

The Cat Car zooms toward the Wolfy Kids, who are flying around, wrecking the city.

The tail on the Gekko-Mobile is hanging low to the ground.

"We've got to get ahold of that tail. It will slow them down!" Catboy says.

"Super Gekko Muscles!" Gekko shouts, grabbing the Gekko-Mobile's tail.

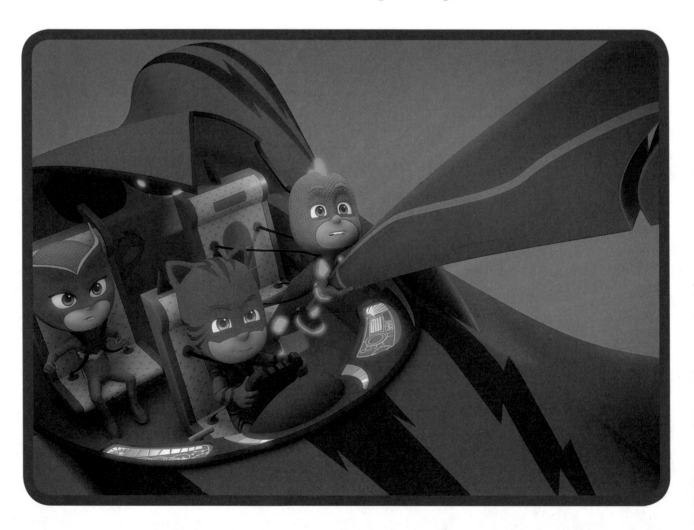

"Owlette! Fly up, release the Owl Glider's claws and take control!" Catboy says.

"But then you'll fall," Owlette cries.

"It's okay. We're over HQ's moat," Catboy says.

"It's not okay for your Cat Car!" Gekko exclaims. "It will sink!"

"The city's more important," Catboy replies. "We've got to stop the Wolfy Kids!"

Owlette detaches the Gekko-Mobile from the Owl Glider, sending the Cat Car into the moat, where it sinks!

Gekko helps recover the Cat Car and bring it to shore.
"One Cat Car safely delivered," Gekko says.
"I have some Wolfy Kids, too," Owlette adds. She tips over the
Owl Glider, causing the Wolfy Kids to land in the water with a giant splash.
"Hey, Wolfy Kids!" Gekko shouts. "You've got work to do!"

The Wolfy Kids are hard at work cleaning up their mess. After washing paw prints off walls, organizing the library, and cleaning the playground, they have to wash the Cat Car.

"Don't miss anything," Owlette tells them. "That is one special car—we couldn't have saved the day without it!"

"I couldn't have saved the day without you guys, either," Catboy says, smiling at his friends.

While the PJ Masks are distracted, the Wolfy Kids escape by running down an alleyway!

"*Yarooo!*" the Wolfy Kids howl.

Catboy shrugs. "New villains? No problem!" he cheers.

PJ Masks all shout hooray! 'Cause in the night, we saved the day!